A ROOKIE READER®

COLLECTING

By Bonnie Dobkin

Illustrated by Rick Hackney

Prepared under the direction of Robert Hillerich, Ph.D.

 CHILDRENS PRESS®
CHICAGO

For Michael, my Mouse

Library of Congress Cataloging-in-Publication Data

Dobkin, Bonnie.
    Collecting / by Bonnie Dobkin ; illustrated by Rick
Hackney.
        p.   cm. — (A Rookie reader)
    Summary: An avid collector enumerates all the
things that have been collected, from twenty-three
keychains and fifty-one shells to a ball of tin foil five
feet wide.
    ISBN 0-516-02015-3
    [1. Collectors and collecting—Fiction. 2. Stories in
rhyme.] I. Hackney, Rick, ill. II. Title. III. Series.
PZ7.3.D634Co   1993
[E]—dc20   93-13021
                                                        CIP
                                                         AC

I love to collect things.
Collecting is fun—

'cause plenty of anything's
better than one!

I've got twenty-three keychains
and fifty-one shells,

seventeen sticker books,
two dozen bells.

GOOSE STICKERS

GHOST STICKERS

ROSE Stickers

MOUSE STICKERS

MOOSE STICKERS

BAT STICKERS

CAT STICKERS

HAT STICKERS

CAR STICKERS

FISH STICKERS

WALRUS STICKERS

BEE STICKERS

POT STICKERS

DINOSAUR STICKERS

PIG STICKERS

PORCUPINE STICKERS

COW STICKERS

9

A bagful of marbles,
a boxful of cars,

a carton of creatures
and pennies in jars.

I've got posters and pictures
all over my room,

models of monsters
and rockets that zoom.

And the bugs I've collected
in boxes on cotton,

are filling my closet.
(They smell really rotten.)

I've got hundreds of baseball cards,
comics galore,

and it's never enough—
I just keep adding more!

I've got three giant suitcases
just labeled "Stuff."

STUFF #1

STUFF 2.

STUFF 3

25

Could it be I don't know
when enough is enough?

Should I stop? Should I quit?
Should I say that I'm done?

Of course not! I told you—

collecting is fun!

WORD LIST

	closet	hundreds	my	should
dding	collect	I	never	smell
ll	collected	I'm	not	sticker
nd	collecting	in	of	stop
nything	comics	is	on	stuff
re	cotton	it	one	suitcases
agful	could	it's	over	than
aseball	course	I've	pennies	that
e	creatures	jars	pictures	the
ells	done	just	plenty	they
etter	don't	keep	posters	things
ooks	dozen	keychains	quit	three
oxes	enough	know	really	to
oxful	fifty-one	labeled	rockets	told
ugs	filling	love	room	twenty-three
ards	fun	marbles	rotten	two
ars	galore	models	say	when
arton	giant	monsters	seventeen	you
ause	got	more	shells	zoom

About the Author

Bonnie Dobkin grew up with the last name Bierman in Morton Grove, Illinois. She attended Maine East High School and later received a degree in education from the University of Illinois. A high-school teacher for several years, Bonnie eventually moved into educational publishing and now works as an executive editor. She lives in Arlington Heights, Illinois.

For story ideas, Bonnie relies on her three sons, Bryan, Michael, and Kevin; her husband Jeff, a dentist; and Kelsey, a confused dog of extremely mixed heritage. When not writing, Bonnie focuses on her other interests—music, community theatre, and chocolate.

About the Artist

Rick Hackney is a San Francisco illustrator and writer who graduated from Art Center School in Los Angeles, California. He has worked at Disney Studios, drawn a syndicated comic strip, and has been an art director in advertising. He has also done some acting, written children's stories, and currently is doing a lot of educational illustration.

Rick lives with his wife, Elizabeth, and a black cat in a home on the edge of San Francisco Bay.